Levi's FAMILY

By Elliot Riley

Illustrated By Srimalie Bassani

Rourke
Educational Media
rourkeeducationalmedia.com

Teaching Focus:

Concepts of Print: Have students find capital letters and punctuation in a sentence. Ask students to explain the purpose for using them in a sentence.

Before Reading:

Building Academic Vocabulary and Background Knowledge

Before reading a book, it is important to set the stage for your child or student by using pre-reading strategies. This will help them develop their vocabulary, increase their reading comprehension, and make connections across the curriculum.

1. Read the title and look at the cover. *Let's make predictions about what this book will be about.*
2. Take a picture walk by talking about the pictures/photographs in the book. Implant the vocabulary as you take the picture walk. Be sure to talk about the text features such as headings, the Table of Contents, glossary, bolded words, captions, charts/diagrams, or Index.
3. Have students read the first page of text with you then have students read the remaining text.
4. Strategy Talk – use to assist students while reading.
   - Get your mouth ready
   - Look at the picture
   - Think…does it make sense
   - Think…does it look right
   - Think…does it sound right
   - Chunk it – by looking for a part you know
5. Read it again.

Content Area Vocabulary
Use glossary words in a sentence.

adopt
foster
instruments
safe

After Reading:

Comprehension and Extension Activity

After reading the book, work on the following questions with your child or students in order to check their level of reading comprehension and content mastery.

1. *What is a foster family?* *(Summarize)*
2. *Why does Levi live with a foster family?* *(Asking Questions)*
3. *How is Levi's family like yours? How is it different?* *(Text to self connection)*
4. *What activity does Levi's family enjoy doing together?* *(Asking Questions)*

Extension Activity

Make up a song about your family. Sing it to the tune of "Twinkle, Twinkle, Little Star." Perform your song for your family.

Table of Contents

Meet Levi

This is Levi.

These are Levi's **foster** parents.

They care for kids who need a **safe** place to live.

Levi's other home was
not safe. Thinking
about it makes him
feel scared.

Levi's foster parents hug him when he cries.

"You're safe now," they say.

Making Music

Levi's foster home has many musical **instruments.**

Levi is learning to play the guitar.

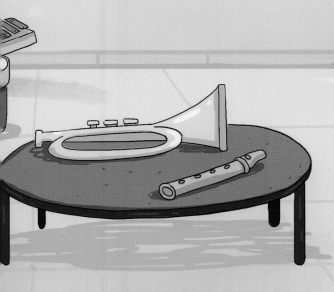

His foster mom plays the drums.

His foster dad plays the keyboard.

"We should start a band!"
Levi says.

"We could call it *Levi and His Forever Family*," his foster parents say.

Together Forever

They show him some papers.

The papers say they can **adopt** Levi.

Levi runs outside. "I have a forever family!" he yells.

His parents laugh. Everyone is happy and excited.

Levi loves his family.

Levi's family loves Levi.

Picture Glossary

 **adopt** (uh-DAHPT): Bringing a person or animal into your family.

 **foster** (FAWS-tur): To care for a child that is not your own.

 **instruments** (IN-struh-muhnts): Objects that are used to make music.

 **safe** (sayf): Protected from danger, injury, or risk.

Family Fun

Who are the people in your family?

Draw each person and write their name below their picture.

How is your family portrait like Levi's? How is it different?

About the Author

Elliot Riley is an author with a big family of her own in Tampa, Florida. She loves when everyone gets together to eat, laugh, and play games. Especially the eating part!

Meet The Author!
www.meetREMauthors.com

Library of Congress PCN Data

Levi's Family/ Elliot Riley
(All Kinds of Families)
ISBN 978-1-68342-317-1 (hard cover)
ISBN 978-1-68342-413-0 (soft cover)
ISBN 978-1-68342-483-3 (e-Book)
Library of Congress Control Number: 2017931166

Rourke Educational Media
Printed in the United States of America,
North Mankato, Minnesota

Author Illustration: ©Robert Wicher
Edited by: Keli Sipperley
Cover design and interior design by: Kathy Walsh